FREEDOM FROM BONDAGE

Freedom from Bondage

By
Anobel Armour

Illustrated by James Ponter

HERALD PRESS, SCOTTDALE, PENNSYLVANIA

1

Frederick carried a big load of kindling in from the woods and stacked it in a neat pile by the side of the kitchen stove. Grandmother Betsy was pouring corn cakes out of a crock into a black skillet. They sizzled on the hot grease and Frederick sniffed hungrily.

She pulled him close against her side with one free hand. "You are always hungry," she said, and she sounded pleased. Then she made her nose wrinkle ϲ him as if she were scolding him. "But you have to wait for the others," she told him. "They are hungry too."

In a few minutes another little black boy came into the kitchen. He was followed by yet another. Then a little girl scampered in. In no time at all Grandmother Betsy was taking up corn cakes for a dozen empty children. After they had eaten, Frederick plopped down on the woodbox. The others worked in the little vegetable garden, but he was the wood gatherer, so he didn't have to leave just yet.

This time he wrinkled his nose at his grandmother. "I notice that you are always careful never to give me the biggest corn cake," he scolded.

To his surprise, something which looked like tears popped into his grandmother's eyes. Then she shook her head, as if to shake them away, and smiled at him. "That is because you are the only one who really belongs to me, like I am always telling you," she explained. "I am so afraid of being partial to you that maybe sometimes I almost lean over backward to avoid it."

"That's because I am the only one who is really your own grandchild, isn't it?" he asked happily. He knew it just as well as anything but he liked to hear her say it over and over. It made him feel so good inside to have a really, truly grandmother.

His grandmother kept right on smiling. "My job on this plantation place is to care for the little children for the master until they —" She stopped suddenly.

Frederick had never heard her say the word "master" before. He was startled. "Who is the master?" he demanded. "And until they what?"

Grandmother Betsy set her mouth in a tight line. "Run along and get more wood," she said. "You know that won't last through suppertime." Frederick knew that she meant it. She let them run and play for hours at a time but when she wanted the chores done — well, she wanted them done right now.

As he turned from the kitchen he heard her mutter something. "Time enough for you to learn the answer to those questions," it sounded like. But he just could not be sure.

The wind was blowing through the trees, free and cool. A hundred birds sang to him. Frederick loved the woods. He always felt as if he owned the earth when he was in them.

"I'll never do anything but walk in the woods when I am grown up," he promised himself. A raccoon chirred at him from a limb. Frederick chirred back. "Do not argue with me," he laughed.

That night they had fried side meat for supper, as if to celebrate a special holiday or something. Frederick liked that but he liked what came next better. "Tonight I am going to tell you a story about the Moses people," Grandmother Betsy said. "There they were, making bricks without straw, under the hot sun of Egypt," she began.

The small black boy who was her grandson settled down contentedly. He knew all the stories of the Moses people by heart but he never tired of hearing Grandmother Betsy tell them. She started wherever she took a notion to start, so Frederick never knew what story was coming next. That made it like a surprise every evening.

Although Frederick liked the woods so well that he wanted to spend his grown-up life in them, there was something he liked much better. Although he liked the Moses stories so well that he bubbled over inside every time that Grandmother Betsy told one, he liked something else much better.

It was a glad something which he liked. But it was a sad something too, because he never knew when it was going to happen. And it was sad because, no matter how happy he was, it always ended before he was ready for it to end.

The something that he liked best of all was the evening when a lovely lady came to see him. Maybe it would be a week — maybe it would be a month — but as surely as sunrise or sunset, there would come a time when he would look up to find her standing in the doorway. And then that evening turned out to be the most beautiful of all the evenings in the world, because the lovely lady was his own mother, Harriet Bailey.

It was a whole week after they had the side meat for supper before she came again. Frederick had watched and watched for her coming. Six weeks had passed this time since he had seen her last. He could tell it was six weeks by the times he had gone to the woods and by how high the vegetables had grown — just like he knew that he must have been born in February because Grandmother Betsy said it had been between wintertime and planting time.

Frederick looked up and saw her and he ran to her arms. She hugged him close. "Where have you been for so long?" he panted. "I thought maybe you were not coming back." He felt her shiver against him, kind of like she had turned cold suddenly. He held her even closer, but suddenly he was shivering too. It scared him inside in a way, because it was so foolish. She was his own mother, wasn't she? She would always be coming back, wouldn't she?

Harriet Bailey smiled down into the face of her son, just as if she hadn't shivered at all. "My work is far away from here now," she explained. "It takes a long time to walk over here and a long time to

10

walk back. And I can't always come when I want to."

"Why can't you? Oh, why can't you?" Frederick demanded, as if it had never been so important to know before as it was right now.

His mother looked at him and her eyes were so sad that it hurt him to see them but she just shook her head. Then she smiled at all of them, brightly and quickly. "I will read the Bible tonight," she said. "And Grandmother Betsy can listen."

They all gathered around the kitchen stove and Harriet picked up the Bible and began to read. Grandmother Betsy sometimes held the Bible in her hand when she told stories but she never once made a move to open it. Mother Harriet always read from the Book and she always read about Jesus. Never once had she read a story about the people whom Moses had led out of the wilderness.

She read about Jesus and how He healed the lame and the blind. She read about how He stilled a storm at sea. She read about how He liked to have children around Him. But the story that she seemed to like best of all was the one about the boy who shared his loaves and fishes. She always smiled over at Frederick when she read that. It made him feel as if he might have something to share too. He surely wished so, because he loved the kind and gentle Jesus.

After the stories were read, Frederick went into the little lean-to off the kitchen. He slept in there on a thin mattress on the floor. On the nights when his mother came, she always tucked him into bed. Sometimes he didn't know which he liked best, the stories or the tucking-in. But most of the time he knew it was the tucking-in.

11

Tonight she stroked his hair and pulled the patch quilt up to his shoulders. Then she bent over him and kissed him. He was afraid suddenly that she was going to leave right away. He knew that she had a long walk ahead of her, but there was so much that he wanted to ask her. There was so much that he needed to know.

"Why is it that Grandmother Betsy always talks about the Moses people?" he asked her. "You never do."

It seemed to him that her face paled under the soft, warm brown skin, but she looked at him steadily. "Grandmother Betsy can only tell the stories which she remembers," she explained. "So she tells the same ones over and over. That is because she can't read." Then she sighed. "If only I could stay with you a little longer each time, I could teach you to read. Then you could read all the stories and poems in the whole Bible."

"I would like that," Frederick said.

"Of course you would, my darling," she agreed. "But I am the only one hereabouts who can read. And I cannot teach you." Her sigh was like a whisper. Then she smiled down at him. "But you will learn to read someday, my son," she went on. "I pray for that for you all the time."

"Is it so important to read that you should talk to God about it?" he asked.

"Yes," she told him gently, "reading is important enough to talk to God about." She hesitated for just a second. "It sets you free," she explained.

"Free?" he asked, puzzled. But she only pulled the quilt up higher and kissed him harder. "Go to sleep now, my son," she said in her low, sweet voice. She was crooning softly to him when he went to sleep, so he didn't know when she left him. All he knew was that she was gone when he awakened and that he felt lonely and hollow.

It was another month before she came back. Frederick was on his thin mattress on the floor, sleeping soundly, when she slipped in and shook him awake. A little candle sputtered in her hand and lighted her face. He saw how intently she was staring down at him, but when he opened his eyes a bit wider, he saw that she was smiling.

"I couldn't get away any sooner," she said. "I walked twelve miles here and I have to walk twelve miles back to be in the fields by dawn. But I just had to see you tonight, my son."

Even if she was smiling her eyes looked so sad that Frederick could hardly stand to look into them. "Is something wrong?" he asked.

"Very wrong, Frederick," she admitted promptly. "But I didn't come to talk about that," she hurried on. "I came to give you a Scripture verse to take with you."

"To take with me?" he puzzled.

"What I mean is," she explained quickly, "that you should take it into your mind now and then carry it in your heart all of your life." She picked up the Bible and put his fingers on the place. "It is Romans 8:15," she said. " 'For ye have not received the spirit of bondage,' " she read.

He repeated the words after her, there in the little lean-to off the kitchen. The candlelight flickered

13

across his face. She caught him to her suddenly and kissed him over and over. It was just as if she were kissing him enough to last forever. He saw Grandmother Betsy over his mother's shoulder. He couldn't be sure in the dim light but it looked as if she were crying.

Then his mother slipped over to the door. As she reached it, she turned and looked at him again. He had the most dreadfully frightening feeling that he was seeing her for the last time.

Lying awake, dry-eyed and fearful, the small black boy repeated the words which she had taught him, again and again. " 'For ye have not received the spirit of bondage' — 'For ye have not received the spirit of bondage.' "

He didn't know why but he knew that they must be the most important words in the world. Why else would his mother have walked 24 miles in the dead of night to give them to him?

2

Grandmother Betsy was standing still and stiff in the dooryard when Frederick came in from the woods early the next morning. A man was standing with her, a white man the boy had not seen before. It was odd the way that his grandmother was standing — as if she were turned to stone — just staring dry-eyed ahead of her.

"Is he a good worker?" the man was asking. "The master is hard on the ones who slacken up along about evening, claiming they are tired."

"He's been carrying the wood for me since he was four years old," Grandmother Betsy said through tight lips. Frederick dropped the wood suddenly and didn't even feel the pieces which hit his feet. She was surely talking about him, but why should this man want to know if he was a good worker?

Suddenly he knew that it had something to do with his mother's night visit. His heart pounded so hard against his ribs that he thought the man must hear it.

"Well, he'll be doing a sight more than carrying wood now," the man snapped. "I hope you haven't coddled him."

Grandmother Betsy's lips began to quiver. "He's just a little boy," she said, and her voice sounded pleading. Then, as if she didn't even know she was doing it, she was brushing tears from her eyes with the backs of her gnarled hands.

The man looked at her coldly. "Stop your sniveling," he ordered. "What are you trying to do? Scare the boy into thinking that it's not good to be a slave?"

Slave! Frederick couldn't hear his heart pound now at all. It must have stopped dead still! He had heard the word only once before but he knew that it was a dreadful word. The time he had heard it was when his Aunt Jenny had been hiding in the woods. He had found her, crouched down behind a stump, when he was running after a butterfly.

"Don't speak out, boy," she had warned sharply, "or they will catch up with me." When she saw the startled look on his face, she whispered, "I can't stand being a slave another minute. I am running away." Then she added, "Don't let on to anyone that you saw me. Don't speak a word."

And he hadn't spoken a word, though he wondered and wondered about being a slave, about its being so bad that you had to run away. Now this white man with sharp eyes was calling him one.

And Grandmother Betsy was trying hard not to cry anymore. It made him turn cold inside.

The day wasn't over before Frederick learned what being a slave meant. They stuck an old straw hat on his head, so that the sun wouldn't bake him, they explained. It was so big that it lopped down over his ears. Then they set him to work in the cotton field. Grandmother Betsy grew one little row of cotton; so he knew what it looked like. But now as far as he looked he couldn't see anything but cotton.

By noon Frederick was so hungry and tired that he thought he was going to faint. When he was handed some meat between two hunks of bread, he reached for it eagerly. But when he saw that it was fried side meat, he thought of the cabin. That made him so homesick he couldn't eat. It was funny because side meat always tasted so good when Grandmother Betsy fried it. The water, too, stuck in his throat at first but he finally got a dipperful down. Then he went back to work.

The sun was going down and all the slaves were using up the last minutes of daylight to pick another row when Frederick fell. It was already dark when he came to, stretched out on the floor boards of a big porch to a big house.

"This young one will never be a field hand," a big voice said from right above him. Frederick looked up into the face of a tall, dark-haired man. He didn't look mean nor cruel. He just looked puzzled, like a man might who had a boy who wouldn't work hard and the man couldn't figure out why. "There are too many of them on the plantation now," he went on.

"It's a job to feed them all if they can't earn their keep."

"He's quite a likely-looking lad though," another voice said. Frederick twisted to follow the sound of this voice and it made him sick all over again just to move his head. Maybe his head had been baked anyhow, hat or no hat.

"How would you like to have him then, Hugh?" the dark-haired man asked.

"Just fine," Hugh agreed. "He must be about the age of my son, Tommy. He'd make him a good body servant."

"All right," the dark-haired man boomed. "He's yours. I give him to you." Then he chuckled. "I hope he makes a better servant for your boy than he made a field hand for me."

"He will make a good body servant all right," the Hugh-man said. There was something firm and cold, almost ominous, in the way he said it.

In a few more days, after Hugh Auld had finished his buying and selling and his visit, they were on their way to Baltimore, Maryland. Frederick hadn't got to tell Grandmother Betsy good-bye though he was pretty sure once that he had seen her peering around a cotton bale at the station. But when he looked again it was only a shadow.

He knew now why he had felt that he might never see his mother again. She must have learned someway that he was to be sent to the fields. She knew that field hands didn't have visitors, and felt sure she was seeing him for the last time.

"But even she couldn't have known that I would be given away," he said in despair as he looked out the windows. Many sights could be seen from those train windows but the boy didn't see many of them.

"How can someone just give me away like I was a sack of cornmeal or something?" he wondered. "How can the word of one man send me from Tuckahoe, Maryland, where I was born, to a place called Baltimore, which I have never seen?"

He pressed his nose against the pane and almost sobbed. "How can a man, whose name I do not even know, call himself my master?" But the questions were too big for Frederick and finally he dozed off.

Baltimore didn't turn out to be such a bad place after all. The house was big and white with large pillars up and down the porch. Inside there were so many rooms that Frederick didn't think he would ever get to see them all. His new owners gave him hot food in the kitchen and he never once saw any fried side meat or corn cakes. Sometimes he got hungry for them, but he learned to like fried chicken and gravy and white beans just fine.

But best of all was Tommy, or maybe it was Mrs. Auld. He could never be sure which. Tommy's shoes had to be shined. His clothes had to be laid out. Oh, there was plenty to do all right but they played together, too. Sometimes he even got to go horseback riding with Master Tommy. Not often, because the groom usually went with him, but often enough to know that it was fun.

Then there was Mrs. Auld. She called the two boys into a big room, which she called the drawing room, every morning. Tommy stood on one side of her. Frederick stood at her other knee. Then she taught them their letters.

The first time that Frederick could put some letters together and make them spell a word, he almost cried. If only his mother could see him! If only she could know that he was learning to read! Then he remembered how she had prayed, and he was comforted. She would know that her prayers were being answered, someway, somehow.

The little Webster's spelling book was a magic thing. It had so many words in it that Frederick knew he would never get to the end of it. Not that he wanted to; he wanted this learning to go on and on.

"It gets so tiresome, standing still and trying to read, morning after morning," Tommy complained. He shook his head and his yellow hair flopped down into his eyes. His blue eyes snapped. "When I am grown up I will not read at all," he threatened.

"I like the reading better than anything," Frederick confessed.

Tommy laughed harshly. "A lot of good reading will do you!" he said, looking at his body servant scornfully.

"My mother wanted me to read," Frederick said shyly.

Tommy looked at him in amazement. "Mother?" he said. "Did you have a mother?" Then he shook his head again. "But I guess you did," he finally conceded. "Even animals have mothers."

Frederick turned and ran from the room. He must not let Master Tommy see him cry. But pretty soon the hurt stopped and he was able to smile. "He probably would be shocked to learn that a Negro boy could cry the same as a white boy," he reasoned. He didn't know why that amused him but somehow it did. Maybe it was because it showed that Tommy didn't know everything, even if he was white.

Days followed days. Mrs. Auld had been such a good teacher that she was actually letting the boys attempt to read from the Bible. To hold the Bible in his hands made Frederick happy, just as he was back in the kitchen on the plantation seeing his mother's hands as she turned the pages to find a story about Jesus — though the pages in her Bible had seemed to fall open to the place where those stories were every time.

One dreadful day Hugh Auld came into the drawing room unexpectedly. He was almost always outside in the mornings; so he had never seen them studying. Now he stood openmouthed and stared at his wife and the two children.

"You can't mean to say that you are teaching this black body servant to read!" he shouted. He lunged at Frederick. In spite of himself, Frederick cringed. Mr. Auld tore the Webster's spelling book from the boy's hand and flung it across the room. Frederick fought to hold back his tears.

"What has got into you, Hugh Auld?" his startled wife demanded angrily.

Suddenly Mr. Auld calmed down a little. "I forgot that your people never owned slaves," he confessed. "I forgot that you wouldn't know."

"Wouldn't know what?" Mrs. Auld pressed him.

"That it is against the law to teach a slave to read," he said. Then he saw the Bible in her hands. Anger flooded over him again. "Surely you aren't letting him learn to read from the Bible of all things!"

he thundered. He snatched the book from her and lifted his arm to fling it too.

Mrs. Auld sprang up and caught his arm. "That is the Bible, Hugh," she warned.

Hugh Auld dropped his arm and put the Bible down, but he still glared. "Teaching him to read is bad enough," he stormed, "but to teach him the Bible!" Cords stood out on his neck and his face was burning red. "Don't you know that if the boy learns to read the Bible," he snorted, "it will forever unfit him to be a slave?"

All at once Frederick couldn't see the room nor Mrs. Auld nor Tommy nor Mr. Auld. It was as if his precious speller wasn't lying on the floor with its back broken and its pages torn. It was as if his whole world hadn't stopped still at all.

For Mr. Auld, without meaning to in the least, had just pointed him toward freedom! Frederick knew he must somehow learn to read the Bible for himself.

3

Frederick thought of only one thing after that. If reading the Bible would forever unfit him to be a slave, then he must learn to read it. Mrs. Auld had been so kind and so helpful. He hoped in his heart that she wouldn't obey her husband.

Because he was so hopeful, he slipped back into the drawing room and rescued his battered spelling book. "I must be ready when she sends for me," he told himself.

That night as he climbed the ladder to the loft above the kitchen, there was a song in his heart. All of the terror of the morning was behind him. "I will be free someday," he chanted. "I will be free. I just know I will."

After everyone was in bed, he lighted his candle and opened his speller. If only he could copy the words he might learn them better. But look any way he might, there was nothing to print on, although he had the box of chalk which Mrs. Auld had given him with the speller. So instead of trying to print them, he read the first five words. Then he repeated them, after he snuffed the candle, until he finally dropped off to sleep.

Frederick helped Tommy get dressed the next morning. Then he went downstairs to the dining room and stood by Tommy's side while Tommy ate breakfast, just in case he wanted anything. The drawing room would be the next stop and his heart kept singing, somehow.

Any hope which the small slave had was blotted out when Mrs. Auld closed the sliding doors to the big room. "You will wait for your young master out here," she told Frederick coldly.

To Frederick's amazement, his heart-song didn't stop at all. It was as if he had started on some great adventure. And nothing could keep him from that adventure, not even the closed door which shut him out from the place where the Bible was.

Frederick knew that Tommy would be with his mother for at least an hour. Tiptoeing out, he scooted from the kitchen to the yard. He was looking for an old piece of shingle or something of the sort. An old, empty flour barrel caught his eye. It wasn't so much the barrel itself which stopped him in his tracks as the chalk marks on its side. Someone had scribbled prices on it. Tugging and pulling, he got it through the kitchen door, up the ladder, and into the loft.

Happy about his secret, he went back to the big hall to wait for Tommy. All that day he walked when

Tommy walked and rode when Tommy rode, but it didn't seem real to him at all. All he could think about was nighttime — and the loft.

Always before this Frederick had hated for dark to come. The loft was lonely because no one was in the kitchen at night and all of the big bedrooms were at the other end of the huge house.

The Aulds had given him some candles and a set of taper-sticks to light them with because he had cried so hard the first night he had stretched out on his thin mattress. Grandmother Betsy's cabin had always been filled with noisy children, sleeping close together.

"It is a shameful thing to have to work so hard to shape a letter right," Frederick sighed as he copied the words from the speller onto the barrel top. It was so slow in fact that it was three whole weeks before he needed to find a rag to wipe the letters off so that he could write new ones.

Learning alone was such a hard job. Frederick might have lost his courage and given it up but for something special that happened. Tommy was sent to school and Frederick was sent to meet him every afternoon.

"I don't like for you to come to meet me," Tommy told him. "It is all right for you to wait on me at home. But if I am big enough to go to school, I am big enough to walk home alone."

"I don't dare let you come home alone," Frederick protested.

"That's nonsense," Tommy snapped.

"It might be nonsense to you," Frederick insisted seriously, "but it isn't nonsense to me." Then he grinned at Tommy because he knew that his young master wouldn't really want him to get in any trouble. "Maybe it is because I am the one who would be punished if I didn't do as I was told," he admitted.

Tommy grinned back at him but Frederick could tell he was trying to think up a scheme. And soon he did. "You walk down the next street," he ordered. "I will go down this one. Then we will meet at the end of two blocks and go home together."

The plan didn't seem right to Frederick but Tommy was headstrong; it wouldn't do any good to protest. Then after two evenings of walking down the other street, Frederick didn't even want to protest any more at all. For he too had an idea. All of the boys who passed him were carrying schoolbooks. Several of them had a Webster's speller just like his own. The next evening he tucked his own speller into his coat pocket, praying as he did so that his plan would work.

His tongue almost stuck to the roof of his mouth as he went up to one of the schoolboys. "I know a word that I bet you don't know," he said.

"Oh, go on," the boy said. "Who cares anything about words anyhow?" He ran off down the street, swinging his books in their strap. He must have had four big, fine books.

Frederick stared after him enviously for a minute. Then he stopped another boy. Just because he didn't have four books was no reason to give up his plan. "I know five words out of the Webster's speller," Frederick boasted. Maybe knowing one word hadn't sounded big enough.

The boy stomped. "Do you really?" he said. "What are they?"

Frederick quickly wrote the five words on the sidewalk. The other boy laughed. "Those little words," he said. "Is that all you know?" He took the piece of chalk from Frederick's hand and stooped down. "I know your five words," he said when he straightened up, "and these five too."

Sitting down on the sidewalk, Frederick began to copy the words on the back pages of his speller. "Say, what are you trying to do?" the boy asked him. His eyes didn't leave Frederick's hands and their slow, painful copying into the speller.

"I have to learn to read," Frederick explained simply.

Just then another boy came up. He saw the words on the sidewalk. "You can't help this boy with words," he told the first boy. "He is Tommy Auld's body servant. You could get into a lot of trouble."

"But, Bill," the first boy pleaded, "look how eager he is. It seems a shame when he wants to read so much —" But he looked worried and his words trailed off.

"You had better come along, Jasper," his friend urged. "No use to be foolish." He took Jasper by the arm and began to propel him down the street. Frederick felt almost as sick as he had the time he had collapsed in the cotton field. Then, just as they reached the corner, both of them turned and waved to him. That made him almost happy, even in his bitterness.

When he reached the end of the two blocks, Tommy was already there. "Don't dawdle along," he scolded, and handed Frederick his books to carry.

Frederick didn't know why he put the speller in

his pocket the next evening. He was a slave. It was against the law for anyone to teach him to read. No one would help. Yet he felt sure that something wonderful was going to happen. He had prayed, hadn't he?

He saw Billy and Jasper walking along ahead of him, but he made no attempt to come close to them. Then he saw Jasper bend down to the sidewalk. *He was writing words,* Frederick thought excitedly, but he still kept his distance. Then Bill wrote some words. After that they went on down the street. This time they didn't wave nor look back.

Frederick ran to the place where they had been. Each one of them had written five new words on the sidewalk. He had to hurry to meet Tommy but he copied every one of the ten words down. Then he ran as hard as he could run.

The next evening he waited for Bill and Jasper. "Thank you," he said.

"Don't thank us," Bill said shortly. "All we are doing is marking our spelling lesson down so that we can check up on each other." But he winked at Frederick as he said it.

"There is only one thing," Frederick begged. "I don't know how to say the words when I copy them."

Bill looked at Jasper. Jasper looked to Bill. "I can't see any harm in us reading our lesson to each other," he said at last. "I can correct you if you are wrong that way." He too winked at the eager Frederick.

Bill stared at Jasper for a minute, very solemnly. "And I can correct you too," he said. He began to read off his words in a singsong voice. Frederick repeated them under his breath so softly that neither of the boys could even see his lips move.

Evening after evening, the two white boys helped him with his reading, though they never admitted that they were helping him at all. After many weeks, Frederick said exultantly to himself, "I am really learning to read at last."

Then he looked very serious and his eyes were almost worshipful. "I have learned many words," he told himself, "but I will never learn any words that I like better than the two names, Bill and Jasper. If I forget all the other words, I will always remember those two."

It was two years before he finally got all of the words in the speller copied and learned. "Well, that's over," he sighed gratefully. "And I guess I never want to see another book."

He kicked at his flour barrel desk with an idle toe. Then he tossed his speller into the corner. After that, he stretched out on his thin mattress, just glad to be lazy. The first thing he knew he was back in the cabin, standing by Grandmother's kitchen stove, sniffing the corn cakes. That was a good feeling and he didn't want to stop thinking about it.

But in spite of himself, he was suddenly standing in front of the cabin and hearing the words which told him he was a slave. Now in this dark, lonely loft, he was still a slave, far from the big bedrooms where the others slept. "No one cares whether I learn or whether I don't," he said to himself. Maybe it was because he was so tired but it was just as if Bill and Jasper had never been. It was as if he had never wanted to read in the first place.

"What is the use?" he asked of the dark night.

There wasn't a sound in the loft and yet he was answered. As clearly as if she were bending over him, tucking him in once more, he heard his mother's voice. "For ye have not received the spirit of bondage," she was saying.

He hadn't consciously thought of those words, which she had come in the night to give him, for a long while now. "Maybe I haven't needed them till this minute," he decided.

Taking a lighted candle end, he slipped down out of the loft and into the library. Prowling around a little while, he looked for something which wasn't used much — if at all. Then, dusting off an old hymnal, he carried it back upstairs.

He wiped off the barrel top and picked up a piece of chalk. "There ought to be enough words in you to lead me to the Bible and freedom," he told the hymnal solemnly.

4

Reading the Bible was the most exciting thing which Frederick had ever begun, even if he was almost fourteen years old before he was ready. He borrowed one from the Auld library.

First he read the Moses-stories because they were the ones which Grandmother Betsy had liked. With tears streaming down his face he realized at last why they were the stories which she remembered — the stories of a people in bondage.

But best of all he liked the stories about Jesus, the ones which his mother had read to him. Even then, it was a long time before he understood that Jesus had brought the world a different kind of freedom from the kind he, Frederick, had always dreamed about.

He never once said anything about people getting

loose from the Romans. The freedom He talked about was the freedom of the spirit. He tried to make them understand that anyone who really lived for God could never be a captive or a slave, not really. For the first time Frederick was almost happy, even if there was much which he couldn't understand as yet.

Then Tommy was sent to school and Frederick was sent to work in the shipyards. He was just a sort of chore boy but there was always a lot to do. Mr. Auld owned two shipyards. Many nights now Frederick was too tired to read. But somehow he didn't mind that for the time being. Talking to the workers was an education in itself.

Watching a man tucking his pay money into his pocket, Frederick asked him, "What do you do with your money, sir?"

The man laughed. "You can ask more silly questions than any boy I ever saw," he said, but he answered him anyhow. "Why, I buy food for my family," he explained. "When my little girl needs a new dress, I buy it for her. It takes a lot to keep a home together," he finished seriously.

The men who took the ships to sea were much different from the workmen. Dressed in their sailors' suits, they hung around the shipyard as if they could scarcely wait to get started on another trip. They had been to so many places and seen so many things that Frederick envied them. Deep inside himself he could not help feeling that a man could be more free in spirit if he was free in body as well.

Sometimes there wasn't too much to do and Frederick talked for hours. Once in a while he had a free day and he talked all day that day. On one of his free days a man asked him to black his boots. "Black my boots, boy," the strange man said calmly. "The bootblack boy is busy and I can't wait."

Picking up the polish, when the regular boy nodded that it was all right, Frederick felt a bitterness well up in him that he hadn't been able to refuse this man. He didn't want to shine shoes. He wanted to dream about far places on his free day, like the places where the ships were going. Besides, he didn't belong to this man. But he was used to taking orders and he did a good job. The man looked down at his shoes and smiled. Then he dropped a coin into Frederick's hand.

Frederick ducked his head. "Thank you, sir," he said. "I will give it to Mr. Auld."

"Who is Mr. Auld?" the man barked.

The young slave explained that Mr. Auld was his master and that he always gave him any money which he earned around the shipyards. Of course he didn't get paid for his regular work because he belonged to Mr. Auld, but once in a while he did a paying errand for someone and that was the money he turned over.

The man's eyes smoldered for a minute. Then suddenly he smiled again. "But this money is yours to keep," he explained. "It is not pay which you have earned. It is a gift from me to you — because you did me a favor."

Frederick looked at the coin in his hand. It was the first time he had ever had a penny of his own. He didn't even know how much it was. Pretty soon, when he got used to the coin, he hurried over to Thomas

39

Street, to Mr. Knight's store.

"I want to buy a book," he panted. There were so many books, it was hard to choose. At last he picked one out. It had a good-sounding title, *The Columbian Orator*. Mr. Knight said the book was priced at fifty cents. Frederick showed him the coin. Mr. Knight said it was enough.

That is how he met Charles Fox, Sheridan, Lord Chatham, and the fascinating William Pitt, his son. The book was filled with their speeches. Frederick especially liked the attitude of Pitt toward the freedom of the French in Canada, and the idea of more religious freedom for people in Ireland. He wished that Pitt were alive so that he could talk to him; but the biographical notes said that he had died in 1806, eleven years before Frederick was born.

Sometimes Frederick walked around the shipyards, saying Pitt's speeches to himself. He liked the sound of them and the thoughts in them. There were a lot of new words in them and that helped him to read his Bible better.

Then when Frederick was sixteen, all of this talk and speech-reading came to a stop. Mr. Auld decided to lend him out. He was sent to work for an absolute stranger on a plantation. His wages were sent back to his master. Again Frederick felt the old resentment at not having any choice about where he should go or what kind of work he should do.

The work on the plantation was backbreaking, even for someone who hadn't been used to lighter work. Frederick didn't mind that so much. He was stronger now than when he had been sent to the fields as a boy.

The thing he hated was seeing the fine young black men who had no hope. They couldn't read. There wasn't a chance for them ever to learn very much because they couldn't read for themselves about the spirit of freedom which Jesus taught.

"But there is a chance," he realized suddenly. "I can teach them." A number of them said that they were ready to learn.

It made his heart ache to see these men, some of them older than he was by several years, as they struggled to spell out even the most simple words. But he kept on and they tried hard to learn.

"We're making progress right along," he encouraged when some of them wanted to give up from sheer weariness. And it really was a hard thing, after picking cotton all day, to hide in a corner someplace and study. Especially when you knew that it was against the law for you to be taught or for you to learn!

No day seemed so hard or so long after Frederick began to hold his classes. It was almost like having a family again, to gather with these men — all of them of one kind and one color. They were so very close to him that he felt as if he were a big brother to them.

Because they made him remember the children gathered in the cabin at night, he tried to do for them what Grandmother Betsy had done for those in her care. He told them Bible stories. Only he did not tell them about the slave folk down in Egypt. They knew enough about slavery as it was. Instead, he told them the stories about the Savior of the world.

It wasn't that they didn't know about Jesus already.

Anyone who listened to their sad songs as they worked in the fields could tell right away how heavily they leaned on the Lord for comfort and support. "It's just that they like to hear the good Word over and over again," Frederick reminded himself. "And I mustn't ever be too tired to pass that good Word along."

When they struggled so hard to learn a new phrase, he spoke to them earnestly. "Never lose heart," he pleaded. "Just think, someday when I am not with you you can read the Bible for yourselves. Now don't tell me that you don't have Bibles. If you want to find out more about Jesus for yourselves you can find a way to get one. There is always swapping and trading." He grinned at them cheerfully.

Several months later Mr. Auld had his "property" sent back to Baltimore. At first Frederick thought that his master had heard of his "school" and wanted to put a stop to it, but it turned out that he was just short of hands at the shipyard.

Frederick still liked to talk to the sailors and the workmen but his mind wasn't on far places now. Instead, it kept running back to the plantation, which wasn't far away at all. "My men will begin to forget the words they have learned," he worried. "But of course they can still talk about the Bible to each other," he comforted himself. "Only maybe they will be too tired when I am not with them."

In spite of the fact that the work in the shipyards was easier, he kept wishing that he were back in the fields, so that he could help his own people.

Mr. Auld kept shuttling him back and forth for three long years. No sooner was the study begun again than Frederick would have to leave. "I can no longer stand not to be able to teach my people," he decided at last. "I am going to run away."

It took many days to slip out food which he could carry with him. Then it was days after that before he dared to leave the field. In the mornings and evenings the slaves were always carefully counted. It was decided that Frederick should make a break while the men were eating their lunches. Several of them knew what he was attempting. They huddled into a tight group to eat. It was harder to tell how many of them there were that way.

After four hungry days of hiding in woods and swamps, they found him and brought him back. "I wish you belonged to us," the overseer told him. "I'd show you what happens to slaves who try to get away." He kicked Frederick's feet from under him and sent him sprawling. "That's a sample," he said. "It's a pity I can't go on with it."

Then, because Frederick wasn't their property, the folk simply locked him up. Mr. Hugh Auld would have to take care of the punishment. However, young Thomas was the one who came for him.

"It's a good thing Papa counts you as belonging to me or else you would be in for it," he said. Then he added, "How could you be such a fool, Frederick? I always thought you were pretty smart."

"Is it foolish to want to be free?" Frederick cried out. Even four days of hunted freedom was hard to lose. "Wasn't I made in God's image, just like you?"

"God's image?" Tommy puzzled. "I don't know what you mean. You have always had plenty of food. Haven't we always been good to you?"

Frederick looked at the smooth, contented face of the nineteen-year-old whose body servant he had been. What did Mr. Tommy know about sleeping in a loft? What did he know about being the victim of a law that said you couldn't be taught to read? How could he know what it was like to be driven by a wish to help others who were in the same situation and then not be able to carry out that wish?

Now that he was older, he often thought of Grandmother Betsy on the day that he had been taken to a cotton field. The terror and the shock had been his, he knew. But the heartbreak had been hers — and his mother's, who was not allowed to establish a Christian home for her own child. What could Tommy Auld know about that, either?

He groaned. It wasn't a groan that Tommy heard at all. It was too deep inside of him to be heard by anyone — unless God was at that moment listening to a black youth who was a slave.

5

Back in the shipyards Frederick kept seeing in his mind the picture of his Aunt Jenny hiding in the woods. He remembered the desperation in her eyes. And something else, too, which must have been hope. "Did they catch her and bring her back like they did me?" he wondered. "Or did she get away?"

He would never know about his aunt — nor if Grandmother Betsy was still living — nor where his own mother was. It wasn't fair. "How would Master Thomas feel if he was taken from his family?" he wondered. "What makes these white folks so sure that it doesn't hurt us — that we have no hearts?"

More and more Frederick resented the injustice of it all. He knew that he could help his fellowmen if only he had a chance. He remembered his students' eager faces and their clumsy, struggling fingers as they shaped the letters which might lead them into another world. If only they had the time and opportunity to learn to read.

Talking to a young sailor once, almost two years after he had been returned to the shipyards, Frederick almost told him what was on his mind. The sailor was from New York. "And he can turn around and go right back to New York," Frederick brooded. "There is no one to stop him. While I can't even —"

The sailor cut right into Frederick's thoughts, maybe because his bitterness showed in his face. "Why don't you run away?" he asked. "Lots of people do. Runaways come into New York all the time, on their way to Canada."

"How do you know?" Frederick demanded harshly, his throat choked up at the thought.

The sailor grinned. "I've taken a few of them across the border myself," he admitted. "I don't believe it's right for one man to own another man."

They were about the same size, luckily. It was finally decided that Frederick would try to escape in the sailor's clothes, using his papers for identification. The sailor had shown his papers once and probably wouldn't be asked for them on the return trip. The hardest thing for Frederick after that was to go about his work as if an earthquake wasn't stirring inside him.

"When you get on the train," his friend advised, "the one thing you must remember is not to look as if you're trying to hide. Face up to anyone who speaks to you."

"I will remember," Frederick promised. But he wondered if he could sit on a train and not look behind him to see if anyone was there who might know him. He straightened his shoulders. "One thing I can do for certain," he said, "is to talk like a sailor. Belonging to Mr. Auld and working in his shipyards has given me that much."

Boarding the train was the hardest thing Frederick had ever done. He tried to step on just as he had every right to. He tried to quit feeling as though a hand was going to reach out and pull him back.

On board at last, Frederick's mind kept running back to the time he had left his home in Tuckahoe to come to Baltimore. Now, God willing, he was leaving Baltimore forever. But it was many miles to Philadelphia and most anything might happen. He shivered nervously.

When the conductor came for his ticket, purchased in advance by his friend who hadn't dared to see him off on the train, Frederick wanted to hunch down in the seat and look as small as possible. Instead, he forced himself to look directly into the eyes of the conductor.

The conductor glanced at Frederick's outfit. "How do you happen to be going to New York on a train?" he asked. "Most sailors don't like that change at Philadelphia. They want to go by boat." He stared at Frederick closely.

Frederick could feel everyone in the car turn and begin to stare at him. At least he thought that was what they were doing. He could not really see them because they blurred in front of his eyes. He made himself answer the question.

"I have been in Baltimore loading a ship for Singapore," he explained. And certainly that was true enough. "Now me, I am not going to Singapore and so I could not sail on the ship." He was careful to emphasize the word "ship," in case a seafaring man might be listening. Only landlubbers ever called a ship a boat.

The conductor took his ticket then and moved on. It seemed to Frederick that it had been hours since the conductor had first asked for his ticket, but he knew that it had been only minutes. He was quite encouraged at the way he had passed inspection, at least for this time.

After a long time he dozed off. Suddenly he jerked himself to his feet and almost cried out. The conductor was simply trying to awaken him, he realized suddenly. He struggled to control himself.

"Hey, there, what's the matter with you?" the conductor demanded. "One would think something was after you."

Frederick fought the way his hands wanted to shake. He shaped his mouth into what he hoped was a smile. "I was dreaming I was in a cyclone off Jamaica," he said. "I thought you were the cyclone."

The conductor threw back his head and laughed heartily. "I've never been called a cyclone before," he said. "I just wanted to tell you that we are coming into Philadelphia," he explained with a grin. "You change trains here."

Just walking from one train to another was almost more than the runaway slave could do. His knees kept trying to buckle, and his heart sounded louder than any of the noisy trains on the busy railroad tracks.

Then the ride to New York was a nightmare. The

closer he got to freedom, the more excited he became. And the more fearful, too, that he might be caught and taken back. He knew the Aulds wouldn't fool with him again if they caught him. They would sell him into Georgia for sure to work in the heat and the swamps.

"I mustn't let this show on my face," he admonished himself. He pulled his cap down over his eyes and leaned back against the seat, acting as if he were asleep. But he didn't dare really to sleep. What if he cried out again and someone suspected him?

His thoughts kept getting darker and darker. When he stepped off the train in New York, he actually looked around for Master Thomas. He was half expecting him to appear out of nowhere to grab him.

But New York wasn't slave country. There were lots of Negroes here and no one paid much attention to him. Even so he hated to ask directions to the address his sailor friend had given him. But he finally had to.

The squat little run-down house was dark when he reached it but he knocked on the door anyhow. The door opened a crack and someone stared at him by candlelight. Then the door opened cautiously and he stepped inside.

"We have to be more careful than ever," he was told. "There has been a regular epidemic of headhunters around here. Two of them this very week."

"Headhunters?" Frederick puzzled.

"That's what the men who try to catch runaway slaves are jokingly called. That's because there is a price on a runaway slave's head and they hope to collect the reward."

51

Only it was no joke really. The headhunters were cruel and dangerous, because they were greedy. Some of them managed to make a good living not working at anything else but selling their fellowmen back into bondage.

A sharp knock on the door startled Frederick. He realized, too late, that a man who had been walking behind him might have been a headhunter. He had seen him but thought he was simply a man going home to his family.

"Quick," a quiet-spoken man told Frederick, pulling a rug back and lifting a trapdoor. Frederick crawled into the boxlike space and stretched out flat. He heard the door click and the scratchy sound of the rug being put back into place.

The pounding of feet over his head was almost unbearable. Someone must be searching the house.

At last it was over and he was let out of the hiding place. "It isn't safe for you to stay here, even for one night," the quiet man told him. Frederick shook his head sadly. He could understand that well enough. "What can you do best?" the man went on.

"I have been a body servant and a field hand. Also I have worked around shipyards for years," Frederick told him.

"You are up North now and only the latter job will do you any good. We will send someone with you to our next underground station," he advised. "Keep going until you reach New Bedford. Lots of shipbuilding going on there."

The quiet man would send word to a "conductor" to come for him, he explained. In the meantime they talked in such low tones that they could barely hear each other. "I am a Quaker," the man said. "Some people believe that slavery is wrong because it is bad for the economy. A white man can't get paid for a job that a black man does for nothing. But the Quakers see slavery as a moral evil, a sin against God's laws."

"I have heard that there are many Quakers in Philadelphia who help us," Frederick said. "I thought about them when I came through there on my way here."

The quiet man nodded. He explained that he had come along to New York because he was needed in this spot.

"I do not understand, though, why you call this the 'underground railroad' when trains are seldom used," Frederick went on.

"So many slaves were escaping and not being caught that a slaveholder said they must be leaving on an underground railroad. We aren't sure that's how the name started, of course, but it seemed to suit us and so we kept it. This is a depot or station; a conductor will take you to the next place, and so it goes."

At the next stop a Negro woman was holding a shivering little girl close to the fire. Frederick went over and put his hand on the child's head. She tried to smile up at him but began coughing violently instead, burying her face in her mother's shoulder.

Just then a tiny old lady, kerchief on head, took the child from her mother and bundled her into a warm coat. The mother stood up, took the child back into her arms, and slipped out the back door.

Frederick was never so amazed in his life. "Should

that child be out in the night with a cold like that?" he asked.

"No, she shouldn't be out," the old lady snapped. "She should be safe at home in her own bed. Only she doesn't have a home and she doesn't have a bed. And the mother has to keep going or she may never have one." In spite of her harsh tones, tears came into her eyes. Though he would never see them again, Frederick admired them both.

While Frederick waited for his own conductor, he talked to the "stationmaster." "Isn't this work dangerous?" he asked slowly.

"Yes," the man answered simply. "But it is dangerous to have the dark blot of slavery casting a shadow over our country, too."

After several more stops Frederick reached New Bedford. It was September 1838. Breathing in the salt air of Massachusetts, Frederick cried out, "Now I am free; now I am free!" Yet he shivered in spite of his joy. Any minute some headhunter might recognize him for what he was, an escaped slave — and that would be the end of his freedom.

6

"When I was shuttled back and forth from the ship-yards to the plantation, I at least got to teach a few poor slaves a few words," Frederick thought bitterly. "Here I am doing nothing."

He remembered how it had been when he got his first paycheck, the first money of his own since that fifty-cent gift so long ago. Slipping it into his pocket, he felt as if he owned the world. But as time went on, his wages came to mean only food and shelter — and he had always had those things.

The words of an old slave named Lawson, who had been one of his pupils on the plantation, came back to him often. "You were meant for something great," old Lawson prophesied. "You are freedom's own man."

As always when he was most troubled he heard

his mother's voice, speaking to him in the dead of night: "For ye have not received the spirit of bondage...."

Just when his mood was the darkest, Frederick read an announcement of a meeting of the Massachusetts Antislavery Society to be held in Nantucket. "It is a dangerous thing for a runaway slave to do, but I am going to that meeting anyhow."

All the men who spoke at the Society's meeting were white men. Though they were sincere, none of them had been slaves. "If I could add my word to theirs," Frederick thought excitedly, "it would make them see more clearly how they could help and why they should help.

"If you stand up and talk, you will become conspicuous," his better judgment advised.

"Slaves can't afford to be seen for what they are," the argument went on inside himself.

"But you might really accomplish something," his heart and conscience insisted.

Almost before he knew it Frederick was on his feet, telling these antislavery people what it was like to be a slave. Being torn away from his family and having no homelife had always seemed the worst part of the whole ugly system to him. So he emphasized that.

Frederick saw tears in many eyes while he was speaking. Quick applause followed that first long hush after his speech. His hands were sweaty and his head was hot and he scarcely comprehended what happened next. "You must join us," the members urged. "You will be a great help to the cause." Frederick nodded numbly.

When he told them that he used his mother's name of Bailey at the shipyards, they advised him to change it, as a safeguard. For now he would be a marked man in public life. Having never been called by his last name, it didn't matter much to Frederick what he was called now. Someone who was currently reading the *Lady of the Lake* suggested the name Douglass; so the son of Harriet Bailey became Frederick Douglass, a name with which he was to make history for his people.

Frederick became an agent for the Society and quit his job at the shipyards. After that he spoke at more than a hundred antislavery conventions.

So powerful was his voice and so moving his story that the abolitionists wanted more people to hear it. But Frederick was in a state of exhaustion most of the time. He just couldn't cover any more ground. Besides, he was worried about a whispered but growing criticism. Many people suspected his story wasn't true.

"He never mentions names or places," they complained. "And besides that, how could any slave, no matter how hard he had studied, talk the way he talks? Why, he is really a great orator. There is something wrong somewhere."

Frederick had been working on a book for some time. He could reach many more people by circulating the story of his life in printed form. It would be a way to squelch the destructive criticism too. Yet he hestitated for a long time.

"The book might do a lot of good," he reasoned, "if the right people read it. But," he argued, "it might also be the end of any work for the Society if anyone from the city of Baltimore gets hold of it.

"I have learned that it will not be very valuable if I don't tell everything, like names and places," he prodded himself. "Yet if I do tell, I will be pointing myself out as an escaped slave." His sigh was so deep that it shook his whole body.

Finally he decided to risk his freedom, hoping that his book would help the cause so much that many others might eventually be free because of the Society's work. The book was published in 1845 — *The Narrative of the Life of Frederick Douglass*.

The first time Frederick saw the notice in a newspaper, offering a reward for the return of one Frederick Bailey Douglass to his rightful owners, he went right on with his speechmaking. The second and third times he did the same, though he slept on an uneasy pillow and imagined figures lurking in every shadowed doorway.

Then one night, coming out from a meeting, he was grabbed by a skinny, yellow-toothed man who yelled, "I've got him. I've got him. We'll sell him down the river to work in the Georgia swamps. No more white man's work for him."

If he hadn't been so greedy, the man might have succeeded in capturing Frederick. He tried to accomplish the feat by himself so that he wouldn't have to share the reward money with anyone. And even then he might have been successful if he had not cried out so loudly.

As it was, Frederick struggled loose. Then before the man could grasp him again, abolitionists ran out from the hall and dragged their fine orator back into its shelter.

It was time for him to make a move, so Frederick went to England. England was stirred up about slavery and it would be a good country for him.

The most wonderful thing about England to Frederick was the opportunity to listen to fine speakers. He heard the Irishman Daniel O'Connell and the Englishman Sir Robert Peel. He met the famous Disraeli and listened to him speak, and he heard Lord John Russell and Lord Brougham.

"It is like having my Columbian Orator come alive for me." He thought of William Pitt and how he had influenced his life. His own speeches had been an outgrowth of his enjoyment of Pitt.

Frederick enjoyed meeting famous authors too. His book had reached England and he was one himself, but that never occurred to him. He was most impressed by Hans Christian Andersen.

"Reach the children, Mr. Douglass," Mr. Andersen advised him. Frederick knew what he meant. Adults changed slowly. But the children might grow up with more love for people of other races.

In spite of the fact that he was so happy listening to others, the English wanted to hear him. Frederick made dozens of speeches. Just as at home, his story impressed those who heard it. The English people collected enough money for Frederick to buy his freedom. They presented their gift to him when he finally decided that he must return to America.

The purchase of his freedom was arranged by a lawyer. For the first time Frederick Douglass was a free man. Many abolitionists thought it wrong for him to purchase his own freedom. They claimed that he recognized slavery as lawful by making a legal deal.

"But they have never been slaves," Frederick reasoned, "and so they can't be expected to understand. As it was, my efforts could have been stopped at any moment. Now I can work for the freedom of my brothers without fear. That is better for me — and it is surely much better for them."

Hearing the fine speakers in England opened up a whole new world of thought for Frederick. He wanted to learn even more. He went to a lecture in the Lyceum in Boston but was turned away because of his color. In England and Ireland he had been welcome. But in Boston he wasn't even allowed to visit the zoo. And most heartbreaking of all, a meetinghouse where he had chosen to go for worship closed its doors to him.

"To free the slaves is vitally important, but civil rights are important too," he decided. "Civil rights, as well as emancipation through legislation, will be my cause from now on." Knowing that a newspaper would give him influence, he organized and published the *North Star*, beginning in 1847.

Frederick came out with editorial after editorial saying that the Union must never be dissolved.

Lincoln's election was announced in the *North Star*. The joyful news of the Emancipation Proclamation appeared in the paper too, and later the end of the Civil War was reported, with the Union still intact.

The Emancipation Proclamation was, to Frederick, the most important thing which had happened to his country, except, of course, the preservation of the Union. With those great goals achieved, Frederick Douglass shut down the presses of the *North Star*, so he did not have the sad task of printing the tragic news of the assassination of the friend who had so often inspired him.

Going into government work, with civil rights uppermost in his mind, the former slave held various important government posts during the period of reconstruction.

When, in 1871, Frederick Douglass was asked to deliver the address in Arlington Cemetery on Decoration Day, he thought it was the happiest moment of his life. Then in 1889 when he was sent as minister to Haiti, he just knew that this was the most important assignment of all.

But when he reached his late seventies, and began looking back, he realized what had really been the most important moment of his life:

"Any success which I have had in helping my people, any words of mine which led to the freeing of even one slave, all go back to one moment. And that most important moment is when my mother taught me the words from the New Testament: 'For ye have not received the spirit of bondage. . . .' "

The Author

Anobel Armour was born in Kansas City, Missouri, where she attended grade school and high school. She spent eight semesters in a school sponsored by the Council of Churches which trained her for church school work. All college and university courses were taken in night schools, noncredit courses in journalism and allied fields.

Before becoming a full-time free-lance writer she was buyer for juvenile books in a century-old Kansas City department store. She lectured on books and authors and also planned all autograph parties, which included hostessing luncheons for famous authors. During this period she taught short story and poetry writing at the local YWCA.

She now specializes in writing story-biographies, mostly about Christian missionaries. These are usually serial or book length, although many articles have been published. She has written *Little Shepherd*, 1950, which sold 60,000. It is now out of print. A book of poems, *In Brief Portrayal*, won the Dierkes Press Award in 1955. It also is out of print.

She is a member of the South River Baptist Church, Statesville, North Carolina, where she teaches intermediate girls. She also sometimes writes and directs Christmas pageants for the church.